D0595966

DEADMAN ANCHOR

THE ATLAS OF CURSED PLACES

DEADMAN ANCHOR

K.R. COLEMAN

darbycreek

MINNEAPOLIS

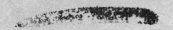

Darby Creek
A division of Lerner Publishing Group, Inc.
241 First Avenue North
Minneapolis, MN 55401 USA

For reading levels and more information, look up this title at www.lernerbooks.com.

The images in this book are used with the permission of: © iStockphoto.com/epicurean (ski lift); © iStockphoto.com/sleepingvillage (snowboarder); © iStockphoto.com/mustafahacalaki (skull); © iStockphoto.com/Igor Zhuravlov (storm); © iStockphoto.com/desifoto (graph paper); © iStockphoto.com/Trifonenko (blue flame); © iStockphoto.com/Anita Stizzoli (dark clouds).

Main body text set in Janson Text LT Std 12/17.5.
Typeface provided by Adobe Systems.

Library of Congress Cataloging-in-Publication Data
The Cataloging-in-Publication Data for *Deadman Anchor* is on file at the Library of Congress.
ISBN 978-1-5124-1326-7 (lib. bdg.)
ISBN 978-1-5124-1349-6 (pbk.)
ISBN 978-1-5124-1350-2 (EB pdf)

LC record available at https://lccn.loc.gov/2015043487

Manufactured in the United States of America
1-39785-21323-3/18/2016

I dedicate this book to Alex and Auggie, whose sense of adventure, courage, and grit inspire me to create characters who never give up.

CHAPTER 1

A storm ravaged the Pacific Northwest. It
rained for two days. A steady rain, a hard rain,
a rain that sounded like the chattering of teeth.
The creeks and rivers rose quickly. Mud swept
down hillsides, and at the top of Mount Hood,
rain turned to sleet and then a heavy, blinding
snow. Three climbers went missing that day.
Kendal and her father were two of them.

CHAPTER 2

The day they left for their trip, Kendal's father wove in and out of traffic. They were late for their flight, and it was Kendal's fault.

"Do you have everything?" her father had said as he loaded their backpacks into the trunk of his car.

"Yes," she'd said, but ten miles deep into Washington, DC, traffic, she realized she had forgotten her hiking boots—boots she'd spent three months breaking in so she wouldn't get blisters. She'd meant to wear them on the plane, but out of habit, she slipped on her white Converse tennis shoes instead.

Her father was mad. Kendal wanted to remind him that this trip wasn't her idea, but she didn't say anything. This trip, after all, was supposed to bring them together—not drive them even further apart.

Her father was an officer in the Navy, and during his last deployment, he was gone for eighteen months. When he left, Kendal was thirteen. When he returned, she was nearly fifteen. So much had changed while he was away, and, since his return, she felt like everything she did disappointed him— her grades, her friends, and most of all, her quitting the soccer team.

For a while, her mother acted as translator and mediator between the two. She soon grew tired of this and decided that Kendal and her father needed to do something together. That's why her mother arranged a trip for the two of them to climb Mount Hood. An old friend of Kendal's father was a professional mountain climber and worked at a lodge out there.

"It will be fun," her mother had said. Kendal thought only a mother who was a former marine would think climbing a mountain would be a fun father-daughter activity.

Kendal often wondered if she had been switched at birth. If she hadn't inherited her mother's thick, curly hair and her father's height and hazel eyes, Kendal would have asked her parents for a DNA test. Both her parents were fearless, competitive, and adventurous. They met while training to jump out of a plane. Kendal, on the other hand, was a worrier, a non-competitor, and happiest when she could curl up somewhere warm and escape into a book. Climbing a mountain was not on her top-ten list of things to do.

"We're going to be late," her father said as they limped in traffic toward the airport.

Maybe that wouldn't be so bad, Kendal thought. After all, if they missed the flight, maybe they could skip the trip completely.

CHAPTER 3

At the airport, Kendal and her father checked their bags and waited in a security line that snaked around and around. Her father looked down at his watch every twenty seconds. He hated waiting as much as he hated being late.

"Take off your shoes," Kendal's father directed as they finally moved to the front of the line.

"I know," Kendal said. "I've flown before."

"Next," the stone-faced security guard said.

Her father flashed his military ID and went through the metal detector with his shoes still on his feet, but Kendal had to put her shoes in a gray plastic bin.

"I'll meet you on the other side," her father said to Kendal, but when she stepped through the metal detector, she set off an alarm because she had forgotten to take her phone out of the back pocket of her jeans.

Her father looked impatient and annoyed when she finally made it through.

"Final call for August and Kendal Gibson," they heard over the loudspeaker.

"Run," her father said, and the two of them ran as fast as they could through the airport. Kendal was still in her stocking feet, sliding across the shiny floor, her father leading the way with her hiking boots in his hand.

"Wait!" her father yelled. The crew was about to close the gate door. "The Gibsons are here!"

Her father grabbed Kendal's hand as if she were five years old and pulled her down the ramp and onto the plane. They were the last two people to board.

A few minutes later, the captain got on the loudspeaker and welcomed everyone aboard. Then he said, "Just a heads-up that there's going to be some turbulence."

CHAPTER 4

The captain wasn't lying. The plane bounced around like the air had potholes in it. Kendal's teeth chattered with every jolt. Her book practically leapt out of her hands. She felt dizzy and sick and spent most of the time with her eyes closed, telling herself not to puke.

Her stomach was still in knots when they got to the car rental place.

"Something with four-wheel drive," her father said to the smiling woman behind the counter.

"Where are you heading?" the woman said as she typed something into the computer.

"Mount Hood," her father explained.

The woman's fingers froze. Her smile disappeared.

"Do you have something with four-wheel drive?" her father repeated. He looked confused by the woman's silence and sudden stillness.

"I wouldn't go near that mountain if I were you," she said in a whisper of a voice. "That mountain is cursed."

The woman reached for a silver cross that hung around her neck and moved it back and forth along the thin, silver chain.

"Six months ago," the woman said, looking at Kendal's father and then at Kendal, "one of our rentals went missing. And you know where it was found?" The woman didn't give them a chance to answer. "In a parking lot at the base of that mountain. The driver had decided to go for a short hike, and he never came back. He was the third person to go missing this year. I'm telling you, I wouldn't send my ex-husband near that place."

The woman waited for them to change their mind, and Kendal hoped that maybe her father would ask for a convertible instead. She imagined them driving south to California and spending the week on a beach. But her father just repeated his original request.

"Don't say I didn't try to warn you," the woman said, typing again and then squinting at the screen. "Just trying to keep my customers safe and the cars returned."

Kendal looked at her father, but her father just shook his head as if the woman were crazy, as if they didn't have anything to worry about, as if Kendal hadn't spent the last month having nightmares in which she fell off the side of the mountain. Over and over, there she was—in a free fall, tumbling through icy, cold air. Nothing to grab hold of. She always woke up just before she hit the ground.

"Come on, kid," her father said, holding a set of keys in his hand. "You look like you need some fresh air."

Outside, there was a black jeep waiting for them. Kendal's father threw their backpacks into the back, and there was the sound of rattling chains.

"What is that?" Kendal said.

Her father moved the bags.

"Looks like someone left us their tire chains, which is lucky because now we don't have to stop and buy them. There's a hefty fine if you don't have them up on the mountain when it snows."

"You don't think this is the car that the missing guy drove?" Kendal said, afraid to get in.

"I'm sure it's not," her father said, scrunching up his eyebrows and shaking his head. But Kendal noticed in the left corner of the windshield there was a parking sticker for Mount Hood National Park. It looked like someone had tried to scrape it off but had given up.

CHAPTER 5

As they drove away from the airport and up Highway 21, they could see Mount Hood rising in the distance. The sharp, black rocks and snow-white peak seemed to want to cut through the silver sky.

Her father pulled off at a scenic overlook.

"Look at that," her father said excitedly. "It's magnificent. Imagine what it will look like when we are at the top looking down."

Kendal didn't want to imagine this. She had no idea how they were even going to make it to the top. The mountain was bigger than she had imagined.

"Hey," her father said. "Let's take a picture."

They tried to take a selfie, but Kendal's father kept making a confused face when he saw himself in the screen, and Kendal couldn't stop laughing at him.

"Do you want me to take that for you?" a guy about her age said as he walked past them. He wore a camera around his neck and a blue knit hat on his head.

"Oh, please," Kendal said as she handed him her phone.

"I'm gonna take a few," the guy said. Kendal's father put his arm around her and smiled stiffly at the camera.

"Wow, the mountain looks crazy right now," the young man said as he handed back her phone.

Kendal turned around and saw that clouds were moving in from the west and swirling around the mountain peak like a plume of smoke.

Her father moved to the edge of the overlook and watched the clouds move in.

"Have you ever been up there?" Kendal asked the guy.

"My dad and I go snowboarding up there every year, but not this year. We're heading to the Three Sisters instead. Every boarder I know who's tried to conquer the Hood has come back injured or . . ."

Kendal would have asked, "Or what?" if the wind hadn't suddenly picked up and forced the two of them to turn away. The cold breeze blew across the small parking lot as Kendal turned back to the guy.

"Hey," the guy said. "Would it be weird to take your picture? It's just that your hair and the light behind you is really amazing right now. I'm taking this photography class and I have, like, a dozen portraits to take."

"Sure," Kendal said, reaching up to try to tame her hair.

"No, leave it," the guy said. "It's perfect." He took his camera off his neck and snapped a few pictures. "Where you heading?"

"To the top." Kendal nodded toward Mount Hood. "My dad and I are going to climb it this week."

"Just be careful, okay?"

Kendal nodded again.

She watched the young man walk toward a baby-blue van where his father waited.

"Kendal," she said before he opened the passenger door. "That's the name of the girl in the picture you just took."

"Bjorn," he said. "That's the name of the photographer who took it."

Right before he closed the door, Kendal shouted. "What were you going to say earlier?"

He tilted his head, confused.

"You said snowboarders have come back injured or . . . but you never finished your thought."

The wind picked up again just as he answered her question. But Kendal was pretty sure he said, "Or didn't come back at all."

CHAPTER 6

He was kidding, Kendal told herself. She wasn't sure why boys insisted on trying to scare girls, why they thought it was so funny. If people were actually going missing on Mount Hood, it would have been national news. Right?

Then again, it wasn't just Bjorn who had mentioned people never coming back. The lady at the car rental place had said the same thing.

Maybe they were talking about the same person?

As she and her father walked back to the jeep, Kendal scrolled through the pictures that Bjorn had taken with her phone. The first picture of Kendal and her father was really good. They were both smiling and the lighting was good, but each picture after that seemed to grow darker. In the last photo she swore she saw a face smirking from the summit of the mountain, so she zoomed in. What she saw frightened her—dark, deep holes that looked like angry eyes and a jagged, rocky snarl.

Kendal dropped her phone. It shattered on the black pavement. When she bent down to pick it up, she cut her finger on a piece of glass. Blood streamed down her hand and across her wrist.

"Put pressure on it," her father said, running to the car to grab the first aid kit from his backpack.

It took her father a few minutes to pluck out the piece of glass and clean the wound. The cut was deep, so he used some Super Glue to close it shut. Kendal's mother insisted that duct tape and Super Glue be placed in all their first aid kits. She'd been a medic in the Marines and used these things to secure wounds.

"Do you think it will still work?" Kendal said, nodding to the phone that her father had wrapped up in white gauze so that it wouldn't cut her again.

"It doesn't look good."

Kendal held the phone like a small, hurt animal and put it in a side pocket of her backpack. She had saved for over six months to buy that phone, even babysitting the three-year-old triplets down the street—twice. Now it was wrecked.

"You need to be more careful," her father said. He was always telling her this. She constantly dropped or tripped over things. It was like her legs were too long, her feet too big. Or maybe her brain was to blame. Her mind was always distracted by something else.

"I know," she said.

She wanted to tell him about the face she saw in the picture on her phone, but she knew it would sound crazy, so she sat silently as they drove toward the mountain, her finger throbbing where it was cut, a sick feeling taking over her stomach again.

They turned off the highway and onto a steep and winding road.

"So," Kendal said, "How many times has Jeremy been up Mount Hood?"

Jeremy was the person who was going to guide them up the mountain. He was an old buddy of her father's. They had met at the Naval Academy and served together on the SS *Carter*. Kendal never remembered meeting him, but apparently he was around a lot when she was really little.

"He's led dozens and dozens of first-time climbers up that mountain," her father said. "He's been saving up and hoping to buy the lodge where we'll be staying."

If it weren't for Jeremy, Kendal thought, maybe she and her father would have taken up bowling instead.

"So he knows what he's doing then?"

"He's a trained Navy SEAL. Believe me, he knows what he's doing. We're in safe hands."

They turned off the highway and onto a mountain road.

"But I thought Navy SEALs trained with

the Navy—in the water, not on mountains."

"SEALs are trained for everything," her father said.

As they drove higher up the mountain, they crossed over the snow line.

"Strange how it all just changes," Kendal said as they went from brown grass and green trees to everything covered with snow.

Kendal thought how beautiful and peaceful everything looked covered in the deep waves of white. For some reason, in that moment, the mountain didn't seem that scary anymore. It was as if her worries were also hidden in a blanket of snow. She wanted to get out of the car and lie down in the white softness. She wished she could take a picture, but then remembered her phone was broken. She closed her eyes so that she would remember how beautiful it was, how happy she was to be driving up this mountain with her father by her side.

But something told her this calmness wouldn't last.

Any second now, her worries would emerge once again from their snowy covering.

CHAPTER 7

"Welcome to Summit Lodge and Ski!" a bright green sign read as they reached a turnoff.

At the top of the hill were ski slopes to the left and the lodge to the right. The lodge looked as if it were made out of stacked logs. A large, wooden porch wrapped around the front.

As they pulled into the parking lot, Kendal saw a police car parked near the slope. A crowd of people gathered around the chairlift.

"I wonder what happened," Kendal said to her father. She looked at the slope and realized it was blank. No one was skiing or snowboarding down it.

"It looks like there was an accident with the lift," her father said, pointing to a place halfway up the hill where steel cables lay on the ground. Off to the side was a tipped-over metal chair.

Kendal felt a cold breeze blow down from the mountain, and she shivered as she gathered up her things.

Inside the lodge, there were a few people huddled around a huge fireplace, hands wrapped around white coffee cups or glasses of dark beer.

Everyone was so quiet.

Her father rang the bell at the front desk, but no one came.

Kendal read the sign framed on a nearby wall: *Welcome to the only ski area in North America open all 12 months of the year. Our highest point is 8,540 feet above sea level. Enjoy the ride down.*

Suddenly, a white-haired woman came down the large staircase and rustled through some papers behind the desk. She looked distraught. Her hair escaped from the braid she wore down her back. Her eyes had dark circles beneath them.

"Good afternoon," she finally said. "Though it hasn't been a good one, not at all."

"What happened out there?" Kendal asked, nodding to the scene outside the large window.

"An accident with the lift," the woman replied. "Thank God everyone is all right, but just to let you know, the slopes are shut down until further notice."

Kendal walked over to the window while her father checked them in. Near the top of the run, to Kendal's surprise, she noticed a lone snowboarder. The sun was dropping fast, but she could still make out his blue jacket as he moved back and forth across the snow-covered slope. It was hypnotic, watching him descend. Like watching a surfer ride a white wave. Her eyelids actually grew heavy. Then, just as suddenly, he was gone. One second she was blinking, the next—all she could see was the blank slope.

CHAPTER 8

Had the snowboarder disappeared behind that line of tall pine trees? Or had she imagined the whole thing? She felt as though she was coming out of a dream-like state.

In the reflection of the window she saw a broad-shouldered man wearing a bright red jacket. This time she definitely wasn't dreaming. The man came through the front door and headed straight toward Kendal's father and wrapped his arms around him.

"Jeremy Jacobs!" Kendal's father said, laughing and stepping back to get a look at his old friend. "I didn't recognize you with that beard. You look like an old man."

"Augie Doggie," Jeremy said. "You look like an old dog."

"Augie?" Kendal said. She'd only ever heard her mother call her father by that name. Everyone else she knew called him August. Or Captain Gibson. Her father didn't look like an Augie.

"How have you been?"

"Good," her father said, then nodded toward Kendal. "I don't think you've seen this kid since she was about two feet tall."

"Ahh," Jeremy said, reaching out to shake Kendal's hand, "your dad goes on and on about you. The apple of his eye."

"Really?" Kendal said. "I thought I was more like a kiwi or banana."

Jeremy laughed. Her father didn't. He'd always been puzzled by her when she said silly things.

The woman behind the counter stepped around the desk.

"This is Marion," Jeremy said. "She and her husband have been running this lodge for nearly forty years."

"Forty-two," Marion corrected. "Ready to retire after this year, though."

"What rooms are open?" Jeremy asked.

"Nearly all of them," Marion replied. "The place emptied out after we shut the chairs down. I'm going to give your friends the Twin Pine Suite. Best view in the place, but it isn't quite ready yet."

"Thanks," Kendal said.

"You'll sleep well there," the woman said with a smile. "And it sounds like you're going to need your rest."

The three of them sat down at a wooden table, and Jeremy went into the kitchen and brought back a plate of nachos, two beers, and a Coke.

"What's been going on?" Kendal's father asked when Jeremy sat down.

"One freak accident after another," Jeremy said, popping the cap off his beer. "Today, the cable on the lift just snapped."

"We've heard the mountain is cursed," Kendal said, stirring her Coke with a straw.

"We've had some bad luck," Jeremy said.

"Mostly, I just don't think people come here prepared. The mountain makes the rules, and the rules can change at any time."

Kendal bit into a piece of ice. The whole idea of climbing the mountain suddenly seemed insane.

Jeremy peeled the label off his beer. "I'll get the two of you prepared. Before we begin our summit, you'll understand whatever rules the mountain throws at us. How's that sound?"

"To preparedness," her father said, lifting his beer up in the air.

"Training begins at 0500," Jeremy said.

Kendal's father clinked bottles with his friend. But Kendal wasn't in the glass-clinking kind of mood.

Marion came over with a set of keys and told them she'd show them up to their room.

"Go ahead," Kendal's father said. "You better get some sleep. I'll be up in a bit."

"Rest is one of the best ways to prepare for any climb. If you're tired, you are more likely to make a mistake," Jeremy said.

"Then I think we should meet at 8:00 a.m.," Kendal said.

"How about 7:00?" Jeremy said.

"7:30?" Kendal countered.

"7:30 it is," Jeremy said. "See you tomorrow, kid."

"Goodnight," Kendal said.

She was exhausted after all the traveling. She followed Marion's swinging, silver braid and with each swing, she seemed to get sleepier. An image of the snowboarder slalomed around her brain.

They climbed the staircase. Kendal noticed that when Marion stepped, the stair did not creak, but when Kendal stepped, there was a loud creak.

"You need to know where to step," Marion said, turning around and giving Kendal a crooked smile. "You need to know the structure of anything you climb."

"Sounds like it was a bad day around here," Kendal said as they made their way to the top of the stairs.

"It's been one bad day after another," the woman said. "The mountain has been bitter this year."

"Why do you think that is?" Kendal asked.

"I don't know, not for sure, but bad things started happening when a sixteen-year-old boy went missing a year ago. He was off back-country snowboarding and never made it back down."

"They still haven't found him?" Kendal asked.

"Sometimes volcanic gas will melt through ice and snow and create a sudden hole where the gas has escaped. After a day or two, ice will freeze over the top."

"Volcanic gas?"

"You are standing on a volcanic mountain," Marion said. "Didn't you know that? Just like St. Helens."

"No," Kendal said. "My father told me we were going mountain climbing, not volcano climbing."

Kendal followed Marion down to a room at the end of the hall.

"There are two bedrooms," Marion said as she pointed to the doors on each side of the sitting area. "I think you should take the one on the left. It's a bit warmer than the other one and the bathroom has a tub."

Kendal followed her into the bedroom and noticed how quickly Marion shut the plaid curtains.

"Why is a volcano covered in snow?" Kendal asked.

Marion began to answer—something about geology and climate—but then said, "The library downstairs can probably do a better job answering any questions you have. There's a whole shelf dedicated to Mount Hood."

Kendal wanted to run straight down the stairs, but she thanked Marion and waited for her to leave. She wanted to go down to the library alone. She didn't like it when people talked to her when she was looking through books.

After Marion left, Kendal peeked out the door. The hallway was empty, so she headed down the stairs. In the lobby, she could hear her father and Jeremy laugh. She thought about how much she missed the sound of her father's laugh when he was away. She wished he laughed more, but every time he returned home, he seemed to grow more and more serious.

The library was behind the staircase and down a short hallway. Books stacked on shelves up to the ceiling, comfy leather chairs, a gas fireplace, and green reading lamps.

Each shelf was labeled: Mysteries, Classics, History, Nature, Romance . . .

Kendal grabbed a few paperbacks from the mystery shelf. She was looking for a book about Mount Hood on the history shelf when a large, red book caught her eye. The color reminded her of a hot coal.

The Atlas of Cursed Places was written in bold, black letters down the spine and across the front. She thought it was strange that there was no author listed. No copyright date, either.

There was a faint smell of cigar smoke as if someone long ago had sat smoking as they read. Kendal looked through the table of contents, and one chapter caught her eye: "The Curse of Mount Hood and Nellie Bly."

CHAPTER 9

Gathering up an armful of books, Kendal hurried back to her room and wrapped herself up in a thick down comforter. She'd suddenly caught a chill.

She opened *The Atlas of Cursed Places* and flipped through the pages until she came to the chapter on Mount Hood. Beneath the title, there was an old sepia photograph. In it stood a short, stout man, a beautiful, dark-eyed woman, and four small children. Rising up behind them was Mount Hood. There was something about these people. It was almost as though she recognized them. When she looked at the mountain behind them, she could see a sharp, snarling face near the peak. She definitely recognized this face. It was the same one she saw on her phone. She wrapped the blanket more tightly around her shoulders and began to read.

Gold was discovered in Oregon before it was found in California, and the yellow metal created a fever like no other sickness had created before. Many of the pioneers who arrived in Oregon in the early 1850s were bent on speculation, including Nellie Bly's husband, Samuel Bly.

The details of their story were faithfully recorded in Nellie's diary.

In the fall of 1853, he and his family set up camp along Quicksand River, a river known to swallow horses and men whole. The river had once run clear and clean, but Mount Hood's eruption decades before had filled the river with rock and ash.

Samuel Bly was convinced there was gold buried beneath the ash. Months went by—but no gold. That's when he heard rumors that a man had struck it rich panning in an unknown creek that flowed down Mount Hood. It was fall by then and getting cold quickly. But Samuel wasn't about to give up. He loaded up his family, and they made their way to the base of the mountain.

Soon their supplies began to run out, and Nellie tried to convince her husband that they should leave and head toward a new settlement that had formed near the coast. But the rage of prospecting possessed Samuel Bly. Even when the snow began to fall, even when they ran out of food, he refused to leave Mount Hood.

Her family near starvation, Nellie Bly took off hunting one day, tracking a mule deer, when a wet, heavy snow forced her to take shelter in a cave. After starting a small fire, she discovered a cache of gold. Nuggets the size of a man's fist, hidden beneath burlap bags that had been eaten away by mice.

It wasn't she who had discovered the gold, but someone else, someone who had hidden it there but hadn't returned.

She put just a few pieces of the gold into her pocket, hoping that it would be enough to lure her husband off the mountain and to buy her children shelter and food.

"Here," she cried, throwing the gold at her husband's feet when she returned to camp. "Please, now let's leave."

Her husband picked up the gold and kissed it.

"Where did you find this?"

"Does it matter?" Nellie asked. "Do we matter anymore to you? Please, let's just leave. We can come back in the spring. But the children need food and shelter. We need to leave before the next storm."

Samuel refused to leave until she showed him where she had found the gold.

"It belongs to someone else," she reminded him as he filled his pockets.

"It is ours now. All of it is ours."

As he spoke those words, the mountain rumbled, stirring up an avalanche. Nellie ran out of the cave and down to their camp, discovering that one of her children was buried alive and that the other children were desperately trying to dig her out.

Nellie began to dig too. When she finally reached her youngest child, the child was near death, her lungs struggling for air. Nellie breathed life back into her child, making a promise with God, with the mountain, that she'd leave the gold behind if only her child would live.

When her husband returned to the camp, she begged him to return the gold, she begged him to leave, but he refused. In the middle of the night, as she listened to her youngest child cough, Nellie Bly filled a pack with the gold and snuck away from her husband and climbed the mountain to return it in hopes of saving her child.

She had only started up the mountain when she saw the light of a lantern behind her and knew her husband was tracking her through the snow.

She climbed higher and higher up the mountainside, her heart thudding against her chest and the weight of twenty pounds of gold pounding against her back.

Snow began to fall, but she didn't stop climbing. She knew that getting rid of the gold was the only way to save her family.

Finally, she found a deep crevice and began to feed the gold into what looked like a mouth. One piece of gold after another, like feeding a hungry child.

Her husband discovered her throwing away the gold and, in a rage, lunged for her. But she moved out of his grasp, and he slipped on the icy ledge along the crevice. He fell into the deep hole . . .

There was more, but Kendal was too spooked and too tired to continue. Her eyelids felt heavy again, like they had when she first saw the snowboarder. It was as though someone, or something, some force, was willing her to sleep. Before she knew what had happened, she began to dream. She dreamed that the mountain was trying to swallow her whole. She could see its sharp rocky teeth and felt its black serpent tongue wrap around her waist. It tried to suck her into a dark, cold, empty place.

CHAPTER 10

"Kendal," her father called to her. "Kendal, are you awake?"

During the night, Kendal had fallen out of her bed and onto the cold wooden floor. For a moment, she had no idea where she was.

Her father opened the door.

She crawled back into the bed.

"You need to get up and get going. We need to meet Jeremy in a half hour."

Her father pulled open the curtains in her room. The mountain was a dark shadow against a periwinkle sky. The sun was just beginning to rise.

Unable to shake the dream, Kendal

stumbled into the bathroom. She splashed cold water on her face and tied her hair into two messy braids.

"I brought you up some coffee," her father said from the other room. "You seem like you could use some."

She took the cup from his hand and took a sip of the black bitterness. After a few minutes, she remembered the story she had been reading before she fell asleep. She ran back to her room. She wanted to know what happened to Nellie Bly and her children. Had they made it down the mountain? Had Nellie's youngest child lived? Was that the reason for the curse?

But when she got to her room, she couldn't find the book.

She searched and searched, pulling off all the blankets on her bed, going through the stack of books sitting on the small table next to her bed. But the glowing red book was nowhere to be found.

CHAPTER 11

Kendal went into the sitting room where her father sipped his coffee and read a newspaper. She hadn't noticed the night before how much plaid there was in that room—a plaid couch, plaid curtains, plaid pillows. It almost hurt her eyes.

Her father looked at his watch. "We better get going."

"Did you see a bright red book next to my bed? Did you take it?"

Her father took a sip of his coffee and shook his head. "What was it called?"

Kendal felt weird telling him the name of the book, because it seemed so strange.

Besides, like the snowboarder on the mountain, she wondered if she had dreamed up the book.

"We better get going," her father said. He stood up and put on his jacket. "Make sure you're dressed in layers. We'll be outside training most of the day."

CHAPTER 12

Outside, the sky was clear and blue. Not one cloud drifted above them.

"It looks like there will be good weather today and tomorrow, and then there's a chance of a storm blowing in off the coast," Jeremy said as they followed him to a steep snowy slope. "I think the best thing we can do is start our climb early tomorrow, so that we're on the peak by mid-morning. Climbing after a heavy snow is never safe. The risk of an avalanche is too great."

"Sounds good to me," her father said. "Tomorrow we climb."

"We'll have to leave here at 0300," Jeremy said.

"Three a.m. isn't morning," Kendal said. "That's the middle of the night. Isn't it dangerous to climb at night?"

"The first half of the climb, we'll be following a trail along the ski slopes. We'll have headlamps to light our way. There is no negotiating the time we leave; we don't want to be up near the peak later than noon."

"Why?" Kendal asked.

"The sun can make ice melt and rocks shift, and it is always in the afternoon when a crevice will suddenly open up."

"Yikes," Kendal said.

"We'll be fine as long as we stick to a schedule and to the route I know like the back of my hand."

Jeremy handed them each a set of crampons and showed them the footwork needed to ascend and descend the steep slope. Instead of watching Jeremy, Kendal was distracted by a snowboarder coming down one of the steepest runs on the mountain. She was sure it was the same guy she saw yesterday He wore the same blue jacket, the same black helmet. He moved the same way, hypnotically, back and forth down the hill.

"Are you paying attention?" Kendal's father asked.

"Yeah," Kendal said.

"Ten points of doom," Jeremy said, lifting up his left foot. "They like to catch on your pants, legs, and shoes. Walk a little bowlegged. Don't walk on edge, but on all of the points."

When she looked back at the mountain, the snowboarder was gone.

CHAPTER 13

They practiced climbing a few feet up an icy, steep slope. Then Jeremy showed them how to arrest a fall using the ice ax.

"Hold it on the top. Not on the shaft," he said. "This point is sharp enough to go right through your skull."

Kendal looked at the sharp, silver point and could clearly imagine it going through her skull, her chest, her leg, her face.

"Hold it out in front, and use it like a cane when you climb."

Jeremy climbed the steep slope in front of them, the ax in his right hand. Kendal watched as the crampons on his shoes dug into the ice and snow. She laughed because he was walking like a duck.

"Pay attention," her father hissed at her for the third time. "You need to take this seriously."

"I am," Kendal said.

"Now," Jeremy said, "if you start to slip, you arrest the fall by grabbing the ice ax right beneath the spike, covering the point with one hand and putting the other hand on the handle, and slamming the point of the ax into the ice."

Jeremy then went into a fall, slid down the icy slope, turned on his belly, and dug the ax into the ice.

"One more thing," he said, standing up. "Make sure you put your feet up because if your crampons catch, you'll break an ankle, or worse, do a cartwheel down the mountainside."

Kendal's father went next and, of course, made a perfect arrest.

"You're a natural," Jeremy said.

Kendal went next. As she climbed the steep hill, her left crampon caught on her right pants leg, and she tripped and fell. Before she could even think what to do, she had slid all the way to the bottom of the hill without any attempt to stop her fall.

"Do it again," Jeremy said.

She climbed the steep slope again, trying to keep the sharp points of her toes firmly planted into the snow.

"Now fall," she heard Jeremy yell.

But she didn't want to fall.

"You need to do this," her father said. "Just slide on your belly and stop yourself with the ax."

She looked over her shoulder but didn't want to go into a slide. She was afraid of the ax, afraid of the sharp crampons, afraid of dying on a twenty-foot training slope.

"I don't know if I should be doing this," Kendal called down to them. "Maybe you two should do the climb on your own."

"You can do this," her father said. "You just need to have some confidence in yourself. And I'm *not* leaving you behind."

She bent her knees, slowly got down on her belly and lifted her feet, and began to slide. Before she could even lift her ax, she was already down at the bottom of the hill.

"Again," Jeremy said.

She climbed the slope again. This time when she went into a slide, she dug the ax into the ice, but at some point lost her grip. The ax remained near the top of slope, but she was at the bottom.

"Again," Jeremy said.

Kendal climbed up the slope again and again, going into a slide ten times before she finally got it right.

"This is a life and death skill," Jeremy said each time he told her to do it again. "It is as important as the deadman anchor."

"I don't like the sound of that," Kendal said.

"Follow me," Jeremy said, and Kendal and her father followed him to a place where there was an even steeper drop-off.

CHAPTER 14

The three of them stood at the top of the cliff.

"You've been training with ropes?" Jeremy said, handing them harnesses.

"Yes, for three months," her father said. He'd made Kendal go rock climbing at a gym every Sunday. It took her a dozen times to finally make it to the top, but she had slowly gotten stronger and faster and her arms stopped shaking halfway up.

"Good," Jeremy said. "We won't be scaling any cliffs, but like I said, we need to be prepared. So I am going to teach you what to do if you need to descend in an emergency and there is nothing to secure your rope. This is the deadman anchor I mentioned before."

Jeremy got down on his knees and began to dig in the snow as if he was digging a small grave.

"You have to dig deep, at least two feet," he continued. "If it's an emergency, you'll likely want to rush this part, but fight the urge. The cleaner the walls, the deeper the trench, the stronger the anchor."

He signaled Kendal and her father to start digging their own trenches.

"Not deep enough," Jeremy said, looking down at Kendal's trench. "You can't take shortcuts on this. You have to be sure it is deep enough."

She dug deeper and made sure that it was at least two feet wide.

Jeremy continued, "Place your ax into the trench and create a sling with the rope. If you don't have an ax, you can stuff a sack with snow."

He placed his ice ax in the hole and signaled Kendal and her father to do the same.

They all stood over their trenches and then Jeremy showed them how to fill them in.

"Starting from the back of the trench, firmly stomp the snow down. Pack the snow good and hard until you have a large block of flat, well-compacted snow all around the anchor. Then give it a couple more stomps just for good measure. You have to be sure that it will stay in place, that it will hold your weight as you descend over the edge."

Then Jeremy clipped himself to the rope and went over the edge of the small cliff, proving that it would hold.

"Do you trust your deadman?" he yelled up at Kendal and her father.

This time, even her dad looked uncertain.

CHAPTER 15

After training all morning, they went back into the lodge for an early lunch. Jeremy showed them a map with their highlighted route.

Kendal finished a stack of blueberry pancakes and four slices of bacon. She was still hungry, so she ordered a side of eggs.

"We'll start here," Jeremy said, pointing to a picture of the lodge on the map. "We'll climb to the top of Powell Point and then onto Palmer's Glacier where we will rest. Then we'll head past Devil's Kitchen and through the Pearly Gates."

"Devil's what?" Kendal interrupted.

"Devil's Kitchen. There's a fumarole there.

Gasses sometimes rise up from vents that have formed in the volcano."

For the first time all day, Kendal remembered *The Atlas of Cursed Places*. She had been too busy training to even think about it, but just then she remembered Nellie Bly throwing gold down into a crevice while steam spewed up around her.

"Hey," she said, turning to Jeremy. "Is there a legend about gold being discovered on this mountain?"

Jeremy took a sip of his coffee.

"There's always stories about gold being found all over Oregon," he said.

"But up here? On Mount Hood? Isn't there a story about gold being found and lost up here? A story about a woman named Nellie Bly?"

Jeremy traced his finger along the edge of the map.

"Not one that I can recall," he said. "Why?"

Kendal didn't tell him about the book. She told her father that she needed to head upstairs and pack, but instead she went straight to the library again.

On the shelf she saw the empty place where *The Atlas of Cursed Places* had once sat. She looked through the other books on the shelf, and read for a few minutes about the glaciers and snowfields that made up the peak of Mount Hood. Apparently, experts believed that Mount Hood would likely erupt in the next fifty years.

She closed that book. That wasn't something she needed to have in her head as she climbed the mountain the next day. No matter how prepared a person may be, Kendal thought, there's no way to prepare for a mountain that suddenly erupts. She thought once more about the book she'd read last night.

There is no way to prepare for a curse, either.

CHAPTER 16

Kendal tried to go to sleep after dinner, but she tossed and turned and couldn't get her brain to shut off. She reached for one of the books beside her bed and when she turned on the light next to her bed, she saw that what she held was *The Atlas of Cursed Places.*

She wished her phone worked, because then she would've taken a picture of the book just in case she was dreaming again. If this was a dream, though, it was a really vivid one. She could feel the paper beneath her fingers and smell the faint cigar smoke.

She opened the book and found the place where she had left off.

Nellie Bly got rid of most of the gold—but not all of it. To her surprise, she started thinking like her husband. Years later she would claim that his greed transferred to her when he died. Still standing next to the crevice, she suddenly found herself thinking about how the remaining gold could help her start a new life with her children. How else would she feed and clothe them? She slipped the gold into her skirt pocket and made her way down the mountain.

When she got back to the camp, her youngest child died in her arms. She knew then that she had been foolish to take the gold. She carried her child and the gold back to the cave, and buried both, side by side.

CHAPTER 17

Jeremy signed their names in a ranger book along with the time of their departure. Kendal's father called her mother to give her one last update. They were about to begin their ascent.

"Call me when you are back down," Kendal heard her mother say. Then her father passed her the phone and her mother told her to be careful, to be strong, and to stay tethered to her father in case she fell.

The moon was bright and high in the sky. The light reflected off the snow.

The mountain was so silent that the sound of their crampons digging into the snow echoed around them. Out of the corner of her eye, Kendal thought she saw something move behind a boulder and then behind some pine trees.

"Jeremy," she said, nodding toward the woods.

He stopped and pointed a flashlight into the trees. The light reflected off a pair of eyes.

"What is it?" Kendal said.

Jeremy clapped his hands.

"Hey," he said in a loud, deep voice. "Scat, cat! Scat!" He looked back at Kendal and her father. "It could be a mountain lion, or maybe just a fox. I don't think we have to be worried, whatever it is. Look at what you're carrying in your hands."

Kendal looked down at the ice ax.

"Besides, mountain lions don't like to go where they can't hide."

"Walk in the middle," Kendal's dad said. He moved out of the way so she could go in front of him.

CHAPTER 18

When they reached Powell Point, they had been climbing for nearly three hours. The stars shone brightly in the sky. It was the closest Kendal had ever been to the stars. She imagined that if she was standing on the mountain peak, she'd be able to touch one of them.

Her father put his arm around her and kissed the top of her knit hat.

"We're halfway there," he said.

"I'm glad I'm doing this," she said. "It's really beautiful up here."

Jeremy adjusted his backpack and looked at his watch.

"The rest of the climb is a bit more treacherous, so I say we take a break and wait for more light."

Jeremy had a camp stove in his backpack, and he boiled some snow and made them hot tea and oatmeal. They ate and watched the sky turn from indigo to a periwinkle blue.

CHAPTER 19

The climb became steeper near Palmer's Glacier and the mountain more exposed. Sharp boulders and glacier ice jutted out in places. Jeremy got out the ropes and tied Kendal and her father together.

"What about you?" Kendal asked him.

"You don't want to be tied to the guy in front. I'll be testing the way, making sure everything is stable. There is an ice bridge we need to cross."

"Where?" Kendal said.

"Up ahead. Just past Devil's Kitchen."

Kendal and her father followed. They went more slowly, more cautiously. It was now a very steep climb, with a drop-off to the left of them.

As they made their way around a giant boulder, there was the smell of rotten eggs. Kendal crinkled her nose.

"Devil's Kitchen," Jeremy said. "Some volcanic gas is being released today. We don't want to get too close to the vent. The fumes can knock you out."

He veered to the left and up another steep slope. When it leveled off, Jeremy said, "Stay back."

Kendal watched him move across what looked like a small field, but when he came back for them and led them across, she saw that there was a deep ice crevice to the right.

Near the peak, they had to climb up and over some boulders, reaching and stretching. At one point, Kendal's father had to hold onto his end of the rope and help pull Kendal up.

The higher they climbed, the stronger and colder the wind blew. When they finally reached the Pearly Gates, they took a moment to get out of the wind and drink some water and rest their legs for the final push to the top of the mountain. Jeremy said that it would take them twenty minutes to reach the peak, and Kendal couldn't believe she had made it that far.

CHAPTER 20

The Pearly Gates were a pair of tall, slender pillars of stone. They seemed to frame the sky above them. As they crossed between the two rocks, Kendal looked up and saw that the blue sky had started to cloud over. She wondered if she could touch one of the clouds when she reached the top.

Jeremy suddenly stopped and looked up at the sky too. He took out his radio and tried to call down to the ranger station to check on the weather, but the radio sputtered out static and then went silent. He turned it off and on again, but it didn't work.

"I put new batteries in it yesterday," he said, shaking the radio. "I tested it out before we started to climb. I don't understand."

Her father took out his phone, but it didn't have a signal, so he took a picture of Kendal instead.

"I can't tell what these clouds will bring," Jeremy said, looking off in the distance. "I checked the weather this morning and no storms were expected until late tomorrow night."

"We're so close," Kendal said, eyes focused on the top of the mountain. She wanted to finish the climb. The summit was just up ahead.

Jeremy studied the clouds and then looked at his watch.

"We're almost there," Kendal's father agreed.

"Let's go," Kendal said.

Jeremy paused, looked back at the clouds, but led the way. There was a clear path to the top, but it was narrow, and on both sides of the path were steep slopes covered in ice and snow. Kendal gripped the top of her ice ax, prepared in case she slipped.

CHAPTER 21

At 10:37 a.m., they made it the top of Mount Hood. To the east the sky was clear, and Kendal could see farther than she had ever seen in her entire life. Off in the distance were three other mountains and, in between, deep valleys and lakes.

"You did it," Jeremy said, pulling out his camera and taking a picture of Kendal and her father at the top—the sky above them, the world below.

Kendal wanted to stay there a bit longer and take it all in, but after just five minutes, Jeremy said they had to start their descent. His face looked concerned as he looked at the clouds racing in from the west.

When they reached the Pearly Gates, snow began to fall. At first it was light, just a few flakes, but then it started coming down heavy and fast.

"We need to stick together. We don't want to be separated in this," Jeremy said. He told them to turn on their headlamps so they could see each other. He then loosely tied a rope around his waist and handed the other end to Kendal's father. The three of them were now linked together.

The wind picked up and blew the snow so hard that it felt like tiny pieces of sand hitting Kendal's face. They had to stop and put on face masks and goggles. The goggles made the white snow turn gold.

Kendal couldn't help thinking of Nellie Bly. Trapped in a storm. Surrounded by gold.

CHAPTER 22

The snow swirled and fell upwards and downwards. They could hardly see more than a few feet in front of their faces as the storm raged.

"Let's take a break here," Jeremy said, gesturing to a place behind the rocks. "We need to get out of this wind, and I have to get my bearings."

"Do you think we should stop and wait the storm out?" Kendal's father had to yell in order to be heard.

Jeremy just shook his head.

"We have to keep going. We have to make it down. If we wait, we could freeze to death." They continued to descend. Jeremy, then

Kendal's father, then Kendal.

Her legs were both cold and tired. It was harder going down. The snow made it impossible to see, and with each step, she could feel gravity and the pull of the earth.

"You're doing great," Jeremy said. "We'll be at Devil's Kitchen in no time and then it's a straight shot down to Powell's Point. Once there, we can follow the ski lift down to the lodge."

They each took a sip of water and continued on.

The wind was gale force; there was nothing to block it. Jeremy signaled them to stay close. He was just a few feet ahead when Kendal heard a loud crack, then a crash. Her feet began to slide.

Lifting her ice ax, Kendal positioned it in front of her and dug the tip into the glacier beneath her to stop herself from sliding. Then she felt the rope around her waist grow tight. She looked behind her and saw that her father was slowly sliding toward a dark crevice. The rope that had connected him to Jeremy dangled loose. Jeremy was not on the other end.

Kendal watched in horror as her father tried to stop his slide. He had lost his ice ax in the fall.

Kendal held onto her ax with all her might.

"You need to unclasp the rope from your waist," her father yelled up to her through the roaring wind and blowing snow. "You need to let me go. You won't be able to hold on if I slip."

"No," Kendal shouted to him. She dug the points of her feet deeper into the glacier. She wasn't going to let her father fall, but when she turned around to look back at him, she saw that his left foot had slipped. In one swift motion, she saw him grasp the carabiner at the end of his rope and unclasp it. She watched her father fall over the edge.

CHAPTER 23

"Noooo!" Kendal cried, but her voice was lost in the storm that raged around her.

Her arms ached, and she knew she had to push herself to more solid ground. She wouldn't be able to hold on much longer, and she couldn't help her father if she fell too.

Moving her left foot and then her right foot, digging into the ice and snow with the sharp points of her crampons inch by inch, she pushed and pulled herself to a level place covered with snow.

When she stood up she could see that a section of the ice bridge had cracked and a deep crevice had formed. Immediately, she knew what she needed to do. Dig. A two-foot trench. She needed to make a deadman so she could rappel down into the crevice. She needed to save her father and Jeremy.

Somewhere in the back of her mind she knew that they might be beyond saving—but she didn't have time to think about that now.

"Deeper," she kept telling herself as she dug. "Wider."

She had one chance to do this right. Any mistake and she would be gone over the edge too. She took off her backpack and pulled out a figure eight of climbing rope. It was bright yellow and orange and stood out against the blinding snow. She made a sling with the rope, attached one end to her ax, and buried the ax, stomping and packing the snow down until she felt sure that it would hold.

Or as sure as possible, anyway, considering she'd never actually done this before. Her training practice with Jeremy was one thing, but now she had to do it for real.

Attaching the other end of the rope around her waist, she got down on her knees and then her belly. Slowly, she crawled backwards toward the crevice.

"Dad!" she called. "Dad!"

But there was no point. The wind carried her words away.

Finally, she made it over the edge.

When she gathered the courage to look down, she saw her father crumpled on an ice ledge. Jeremy lay a few feet away, his body still.

"Dad! Answer me if you can hear me. Say something—*please*!"

The wind howled in her ears. She couldn't hear his voice, but she saw him attempt to get up.

"Don't move!" she yelled as loud as she could. He was perilously close to the edge. "Just stay there. I'm coming down."

CHAPTER 24

Slowly, she lowered herself down, using her feet to push off against the glacier wall.

"Kendal," her father said when she was just a few feet away.

"Don't move," she repeated. There was only a few feet of slack in the rope, so she had to unharness herself in order to reach her dad.

"Are you hurt?" she said to her father.

"My leg," he said.

She saw the pain in his face and guessed his leg was broken. "We need to get you out of here."

"You should leave. Go down the mountain and get help."

It was icy cold in the crevice, like entering a deep freeze. If she left, her father would freeze to death.

"What about Jeremy?" her father asked.

"I don't know," she said.

She crawled over to Jeremy and was happy when she saw him move, try to sit up. For a second she thought that maybe he was okay. That's when she saw the blood on the top of his head.

CHAPTER 25

Kendal found the first aid kit in her father's pack. She wrapped his leg with duct tape to help stabilize the bone. Next up was the cut on Jeremy's head. Kendal cleaned the large gash, then sealed it with Super Glue. The head injury was bad. He couldn't focus when he opened his eyes and seemed to fade in and out of consciousness.

"I'm going to climb back up and help pull you out," Kendal told her father. "And then I'll go back for Jeremy."

Kendal dug the points of her crampons into the glacier wall and pulled herself up with the rope. It was nothing like climbing the plastic

wall back at the gym near their house, but
at least her arms were strong enough to pull
herself to the top.

When she was over the edge, she threw the
rope down to her father. She couldn't see him,
but she knew that he was pulling himself slowly
up, pushing off the ice with his one good leg.
When she saw him reach over the ledge, she
pulled him up with all her might until he was
safely next to her.

Jeremy was next. How were they going to
rescue a barely conscious man?

CHAPTER 26

The only way to save Jeremy, Kendal realized, was to go back into the gorge.

This time, she took an extra rope with her.

"I'm so cold," Jeremy said. His lips were blue. His skin was white, emptied of all color.

"We're going to get you out," she said.

He closed his eyes again.

"Stay with me," she said. "You're a Navy SEAL. You can't give up. You can't surrender. You have to keep going."

Kendal moved him into a sitting position, and as she did so, her headlamp shined over the ledge and caught on something another twenty feet down. She steadied the light and saw that there was another body—a body wrapped in a blue ski jacket.

She nearly fell over the edge, but caught hold of Jeremy's arm and balanced herself.

"Jeremy," she said. "I need you to stay here for a second. Don't move." She crawled on her belly and looked over the edge again. This time she could clearly see the body below. It was perfectly preserved, frozen. Next to it, there was a snowboard, cracked in two.

There was nothing Kendal could do for the snowboarder—he was already gone. She concentrated instead on Jeremy and getting him out of there alive. She turned his backpack into a harness. Kendal and her father would have to pull him out.

When she had the rope secured around Jeremy, she climbed back out of the crevice again. Then she and her father slowly pulled Jeremy out of the crevice and over the ledge.

Jeremy was shaking. They needed shelter, and they needed it fast.

CHAPTER 21

Kendal pulled her ice ax from its shallow grave. That's when she spotted the cave. Only thirty feet away. She sighed with relief— except . . . the entrance. It was covered in snow. For the first time, Kendal felt like giving up. The nonstop blizzard. Her achy, dead-tired muscles. It was all too much. She could feel drops of sweat turn to ice. Any second now, her body would be wracked with shivering spasms.

She cursed because there was nothing else to do. She kicked the snow for the same reason. Then she kicked it again. And again. At least it would keep her body temperature up.

Her boots swept through the snow, over and over. Until they didn't.

The toe of her boot thudded against something. Something hard. Ice? She looked down.

It was a backpack, still partially buried.

It must have belonged to the body down in the crevice. Kendal handled the backpack as though it was a sacred thing. The buckles were frozen shut. If she could thaw them out and open the pack, maybe she'd find supplies.

"Kendal?" her father said. "Where are you going?"

"To get us into that cave," she said.

CHAPTER 28

Which is exactly what she did.

All she had was her ax and her hands, but they were enough. She hacked away at the snow; she scraped and scooped it. She didn't realize her hands had completely frozen until the three of them were inside the cave. The warmth made her fingers throb.

"Where'd you get that extra pack?" her father asked.

She told him she found it buried in the snow, but she didn't tell him about the body in the crevice. He was in enough pain already. She didn't want to give him anything else to worry about.

Still, the backpack might prove to be a lifesaver. Literally. The buckles were still frozen, which was weird. Shouldn't they have thawed by now? It was almost as if the backpack didn't want to be opened.

Near the entrance to the cave, Kendal set up the propane stove from Jeremy's pack. She melted snow for them to drink. The heat of the blue flame warmed her fingers and face and sent more heat down into the small snow cave.

Jeremy opened his eyes again and was able to sit up and drink a few sips of tea and swallow a crushed pain reliever.

"Where am I?" he said.

"You're on the mountain," her father said. "But we're safe thanks to Kendal."

"Thanks to the deadman anchor," Kendal said.

"Radio for help," Jeremy said.

"We tried," her father said.

The radio was broken. Kendal had watched her father try to fix it, perhaps a way to distract himself from the pain, but the radio never turned on. They tried her father's phone too, but after a couple attempts the battery died. And Jeremy had no phone, because he had brought the radio instead.

Time slowly passed in the cave. There was nothing they could do but wait. Wait and think. It only now occurred to her that Nellie Bly's family had been stuck in a cave as well. Where had the story said they were on the mountain again? She couldn't remember. Was it possible that *this* was the exact same cave?

No, that would be impossible. There must be dozens (or hundreds? or even thousands?) of caves in the mountain. Right?

"It's getting late," her father said, bringing Kendal out of her thoughts.

"I wish we could call Mom and let her know we are okay," she said. They were supposed to be down from the mountain by early afternoon. Her mother would have called the ranger station and ordered a rescue team by now.

"Your mom knows we're fine," Kendal's father said. "I sent her a message just now. I used to do it all the time on the ship. Letting her know when I couldn't call her that I was all right, that I was thinking of her and you—I sent it with my heart and mind."

Kendal crawled next to her father and the two of them fell asleep.

The next morning, Kendal had to dig herself out of the cave. The entire opening had once again filled up with snow. When she finally cleared out the door, she hoped to see that the snow had stopped, but it hadn't. She could only see about six feet away.

Kendal knew she had to at least mark where they were so she positioned her bright red backpack outside the front door. Would that be enough? Would a rescue team spot the pack?

The snow was still practically blinding. She seriously doubted a puny backpack would do the trick.

Maybe she could construct some other type of signal? Or make a trail to the cave?

She had to do something; she'd sat around long enough.

Soon, the propane would run out. So would the food and the medicine.

"I should go for help," Kendal said to her father.

To her surprise, her father didn't object. Instead, he said, "I'm sorry I dragged you up this mountain, kid. I should have listened to you. A beach vacation. That's what we're going to do when we get off this mountain. Sit on a warm beach in the sun."

Kendal smiled at this.

When her father turned back to Jeremy, she went over to the small backpack. Finally, she was able to unbuckle it. She dumped the contents out on her lap. There was a bright red climbing rope. A frozen phone. And some . . . rocks? But why would someone carry rocks in their pack? Wouldn't they just weigh the person down? She turned on her headlamp and saw that these were not rocks.

They were gold.

Gold nuggets, to be precise. Some of them the size of her fist.

Nellie Bly's cursed gold. She was sure of it. The snowboarder had somehow found it and made the mistake of trying to leave the mountain with it.

Kendal wouldn't make the same mistake.

CHAPTER 29

She quickly put the gold back in the backpack. Was she crazy, or could she actually feel the bad luck crawling over her arms as she buckled the bag? Quickly, she threw the backpack back outside.

"What was that about?" her father asked.

"Nothing," she lied. "I dumped out all the useful supplies, so I thought we could use the bag as another signal."

She couldn't tell him the truth. For one thing, he'd never believe her. And what if he did? What if he didn't believe her about the curse, but wanted to keep the gold?

Kendal couldn't take that chance.

"I thought you wanted to go for help," her father said.

"Maybe tomorrow," she said. Right at this moment, she felt too spooked to follow the cursed backpack outside.

Her dad looked confused, but he didn't press. He wasn't about to complain about his daughter *not* risking her life.

But that night, she couldn't stop thinking about the gold. She thought about how Jeremy could buy the lodge with the gold, fix it up, and make it great again. Then she thought how the gold would allow her father to retire from the Navy. He'd never have to go out to sea for months at a time again. The gold could make them happy. She even started to crawl toward the entrance of the cave, her movements steady, trancelike.

"Kendal?"

It was her father.

She snapped her heavy eyelids open.

"You okay?" he asked.

"I am now," she said.

At least I think I am, she said to herself. *Or has the curse already set in?*

CHAPTER 30

The next morning, light fell through the cave entrance. The wind and snow had finally let up a little.

Maybe the curse had calmed down? Could curses do that? If so, what would make a curse less angry? Kendal thought about the backpack filled with gold. Maybe the curse liked that she threw the bag aside? Or that she resisted—thanks to her dad—going back to get it?

Maybe.

There was no way to know for sure.

"How's Jeremy?" she asked her father.

"Not good," her father said. He limped across the cave and joined her by the entrance.

"Now or never," Kendal said.

Her father understood. "You're going out for help."

She nodded but didn't say anything. They both looked out at still-falling snow. Behind them were the Pearly Gates, below was Devil's Kitchen, and just to her left was the crevice where the ice bridge had given way.

Kendal saw that there was a flat, wide-open space near Devil's Kitchen, a good place to put a signal for help.

She gathered up the climbing rope and started to hike through the deep snow. On an impulse, she turned around and grabbed the backpack filled with the gold. She wanted to carry it far, far away.

Evidently, the curse didn't understand her motives, because instantly the blizzard resumed. She thought about returning to the cave, but thought better of it. They needed to send a signal, and she was the only one healthy enough to do it.

The icy wind picked up as she hiked through the deep snow. Kendal's legs grew tired quickly. Her eyes watered. The backpack seemed to be getting heavier and heavier. It took all her strength to remain upright.

When she reached the open snow field, she unwound the rope and used it to form the letters: SOS. It stood out against the white snow. It would signal that they were still alive.

Assuming, of course, the blizzard let up. Right now, rescuers would be lucky to see a few feet in front of their faces.

By now, the backpack felt as though it were filled with anvils. Kendal shrugged the pack off her shoulders. The moment she did, the snow abated. Not a lot, but some. Kendal could see ten feet in front of her instead of two.

Her eyes moved back and forth from the backpack to the cliff from which her father had fallen.

And right then Kendal knew what to do.

Instead of returning to the snow cave, she grabbed hold of the backpack. Instantly, the snowfall increased. The backpack was now too heavy to carry, so Kendal dragged it through the snow. As she did, she thought about Nellie Bly. She sniffed the icy air. The scent was faint at first, but it grew stronger. Rotten eggs. Thanks to the unrelenting snow and the weight of the bag, her progress was slow. But, eventually, she made it. The vent in the ground. The place where warm, volcanic air escaped, creating a deep crevice. The place where Nellie Bly had dumped the gold.

Well, most of it.

Kendal was determined to finish the deed.

She covered her nose and mouth with her face mask and crawled on her belly until she was close enough to throw each and every piece of gold from the backpack deep into the gaseous crevice.

CHAPTER 31

Kendal was back in the cave, trying to get Jeremy to chew on a piece of ice, when she heard the sound of a helicopter.

She scrambled out of the cave and waved her arms and jumped up and down.

"Here!" she shouted to the empty sky. "Here!"

A Black Hawk helicopter rose over a ridge and hovered above the place where she had placed the SOS.

Two rescuers descended from the helicopter.

They removed her father first and then Jeremy.

There was no place for the helicopter to land, so Jeremy and her father had to be lifted up in a basket.

"We're lucky that blizzard finally stopped," her dad said to Kendal before he was lifted away.

It takes more than luck to lift a curse, Kendal thought.

"You're next," the rescuer said to her.

"There's another body," she said, pointing to the crevice a few feet away. "Down there. I'm sure it's the snowboarder who went missing."

"We'll come back for him," the rescuer said. "Today we take care of the living."

They loaded Kendal into the helicopter and they flew down the mountain, over the ski slope. The sun was just beginning to set when Kendal spotted the snowboarder again. This time, he stopped and waved at her. Then his blue jacket faded to white and he disappeared.

CHAPTER 32

Kendal's mother was already at the hospital when they arrived.

"They had to hold me back from climbing up that mountain to look for you," her mother said, gripping Kendal in her arms.

"Didn't you get our message?" Kendal said, smiling at her dad as he sat up in his hospital bed. "We tried to tell you we were fine."

"I knew that you two were strong," her mother said. "I knew that you would fight to survive."

"Your daughter was the one who saved us," her father said.

"It wasn't just me," Kendal said. "The deadman anchor helped haul you out too."

"Jeremy prepared us well," her father said.

"How is he?" Kendal said.

"He's going to be just fine," her father said. "Thanks to you."

CHAPTER 33

After a couple days, Kendal's father and Jeremy were released from the hospital, and they all headed back up to the Summit Lodge to gather up their things.

When they turned into the parking lot, Kendal was glad to see that the chairlifts were running again, that the ski slopes were covered once more with skiers and snowboarders.

Marion gave Kendal a huge hug and made them all sit down in front of the fire.

Someone handed Kendal a mug of hot chocolate, and when she looked up, she saw that it was Bjorn, the guy who had taken her picture near the scenic overlook.

"Hey," he said.

"Hey," she replied, surprised to see him again.

He sat down next to her near the fireplace.

"I'm glad you're okay. My dad and I came up to help with the rescue, but I hear you rescued yourself."

"With a little help from a Black Hawk helicopter," Kendal said.

Bjorn smiled. "I kept thinking of you after we drove away. I'm so glad you're okay."

"I am," Kendal said. "I'm good."

"Thought you should have this."

He handed her a framed copy of the picture he'd taken at the scenic overlook. Her hair swirled around her head. Mount Hood rose up behind her.

For as long as she could remember, she'd been self-conscious about her hair. Only a few days ago this picture would have horrified her.

But now? Now she kind of liked it whipping in the wind.

"Someday I want to learn to snowboard," she blurted out for some reason.

"I could teach you today. This afternoon."

"I'd like that," Kendal said.

She went up to her room to change and saw that someone had straightened up for her. The bed was neatly made. On the pillow sat the red-covered book—*The Atlas of Cursed Places*. She picked it up. The book's heft was chilling. Could there really be this many cursed places?

It was also exciting.

All over the world there were dangers to be conquered, mysteries to be solved.

SEEK THE TRUTH AND FIND THE CAUSE
WITH
THE PARANORMALISTS

CASE 1:
THE HAUNTING OF APARTMENT 101

Jinx was a social reject who became a punked-out paranormal investigator. Jackson is a jock by day and Jinx's ghost-hunting partner by night. When a popular girl named Emily asks the duo to explore a haunting in her dad's apartment, Jinx is skeptical—but Jackson insists they take the case. And the truth they find is even stranger than Emily's story.

CASE 2:
THE TERROR OF BLACK EAGLE TAVERN

Jinx's ghost-hunting partner Jackson may be a jock, but Jinx is not interested in helping his football buddy Todd—until Todd's case gets too weird to ignore. A supernatural presence is causing chaos at the bar Todd's family owns. And the threat has a connection to Todd that's deeper than even he realizes . . .

CASE 3:
THE MAYHEM ON MOHAWK AVENUE

Jinx and Jackson have become the go-to ghost hunters at their high school. When a new kid in town tries to get in on their business, Jinx is furious. Portland only needs one team to track down ghosties! But Jinx's quest to shut down her competition will lead her and Jackson down a dangerous path . . .

CASE 4:
THE BRIDGE OF DEATH

Jinx is the top paranormal investigator at her high school, and she has a blog to prove it. Jackson's her ghost-hunting partner by night—former partner, anyway. After a shakeup in the Paranormalists' operation, the two ex–best friends are on the outs, and at the worst possible time. Because a deadly supernatural threat is putting their classmates in harm's way . . .

ABOUT THE AUTHOR

K. R. Coleman is a writer and teacher. She loves teaching students how to tell a scary story at the Loft Literary Center. Her writing has been published in *Crab Orchard Review, Paper Darts, McSweeney's Internet Tendencies, Canvas,* and *Revolver.* She is a recent winner of the 2014-2015 Loft Mentor Series and Minnesota Emerging Writers' Grant. She lives in South Minneapolis with her husband, two boys, and a dog named Happy.